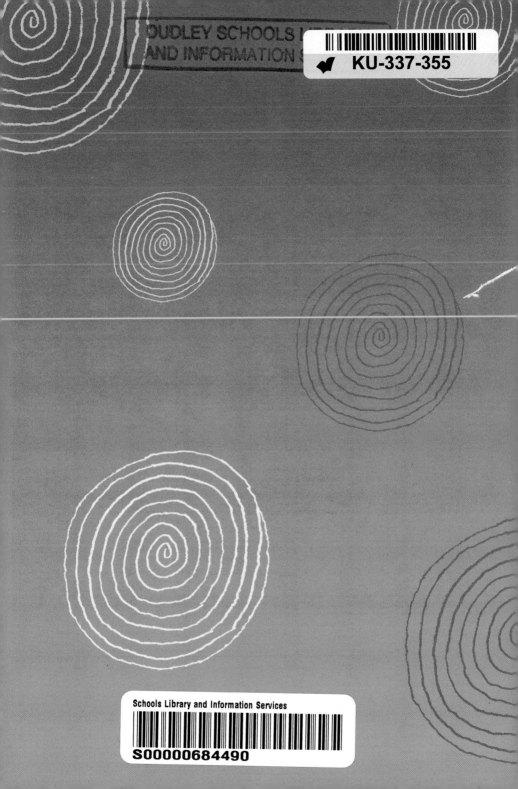

MONSTER AND Frog

MIND THE BABY

For Lily
R.I.

For Elaine
R.A.

Consultant: Prue Goodwin,
Lecturer in literacy and children's books,
University of Reading

ORCHARD BOOKS
338 Euston Road, London NW1 3BH
Orchard Books Australia
Hachette Children's Books
Level 17/207 Kent Street, Sydney NSW 2000

First published in Great Britain in 2006
First paperback publication 2007

A CIP catalogue record for this book is available from the British Library

ISBN 1 84121 544 9 (hardback)
ISBN 1 84362 232 7 (paperback)

1 3 5 7 9 10 8 6 4 2

Printed in China

MONSTER AND Frog

MIND THE BABY

ROSE IMPEY   RUSSELL AYTO

ORCHARD BOOKS

Monster's sister has to go out.
She asks Monster to look after
her baby.

Monster has never looked after
a baby before.

"Do not worry," says Monster's
sister. "My baby never cries."

The baby falls asleep. The house is quiet.

Suddenly, there is a loud knock at the door.

Frog has come to help look after
the baby. "Anybody in?" he shouts.

Frog has woken the baby.
She starts to cry.

"Do not worry," says Frog.
"I know all about babies."

Frog picks up the baby.
"This baby is leaking," he says.
"Her nappy needs changing."

Monster has never changed
a nappy before.
"Leave it to me," says Frog.
"I am an expert on nappies."

Frog wraps the baby in
a new nappy.

But now the baby looks more like
a parcel.

"I do not think that is right,"
says Monster.
"Just practising," says Frog.

He tries again. This time the
baby looks more like a mummy.

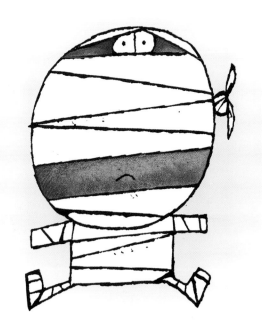

"Nappies are not as easy as they
look," says Frog.

Monster tries this time.

"That is better," he says.

But even with a new nappy the baby
is still crying.

"That is funny," says Monster.
"My sister says that her baby
never cries."
"She is hungry," says Frog.
"Trust me. I know everything
about babies."

Monster gives the baby a bottle
of milk.
The baby drinks it all up.

Glug-glug-glug.

"I told you she was hungry,"
says Frog.

But soon the baby is
crying again.
"I do not understand," says
Monster. "This baby never cries."

"This baby needs burping,"
says Frog. "And luckily
I am an expert at burping
babies."

Frog puts the baby over
his shoulder.
He pats her on the back.
The baby gives a big burp.

Then another . . .

The baby smiles.

Monster and Frog smile too.

At last the baby stops crying.

But not for long.

Waah!

"This baby is bored," says Frog.
"She wants to play."
Monster has never played with
a baby before.

He pulls funny faces . . .

and gives her a ride on his knee.

Jiggity-jig!

But the baby *still* cries.

Now Monster is worn out.
"Leave this to me," says Frog.
"Playing with babies is
my speciality."

Frog tickles the baby's tummy.

Cuchi-cuchi-coo.

Then, he sings to her.

Croak! Croak!

But Frog's singing makes the baby cry more than ever.

Monster looks as if he might
cry too.

"Do not worry," says Frog.
"I will think of something.
I am full of ideas."

But Monster has had enough.
He puts the baby back in her cot.

"What is this?" he says.

"That is a dummy," says Frog.
"What is it for?" asks Monster.
But Frog does not seem to be an
expert on dummies.

Monster tries the dummy in the baby's mouth.

At long last the baby stops crying. The house is quiet again.

Just then Monster's sister
comes home.

"You see? I told you, my baby
never cries," she says. "As long as
she has her dummy."

"Yes," says Frog. "That is just what I told Monster. It is a good job I was here. I am an expert on babies."

MONSTER AND Frog

ROSE IMPEY   RUSSELL AYTO

Enjoy all these adventures with Monster and Frog!

Monster and Frog and the Big Adventure
ISBN 1 84121 536 8
Monster and Frog Get Fit
ISBN 1 84121 542 2
Monster and Frog and the Slippery Wallpaper
ISBN 1 84121 540 6
Monster and Frog Mind the Baby
ISBN 1 84121 544 9
Monster and Frog and the Terrible Toothache
ISBN 1 84121 534 1
Monster and Frog and the All-in-Together Cake
ISBN 1 84121 546 5
Monster and Frog and the Haunted Tent
ISBN 1 84121 538 4
Monster and Frog and the Magic Show
ISBN 1 84121 548 1

All priced at £8.99

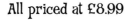

Orchard Colour Crunchies are available from all good bookshops, or can be ordered
direct from the publisher: Orchard Books, PO BOX 29, Douglas IM99 1BQ
Credit card orders please telephone 01624 836000
or fax 01624 837033 or visit our Internet site: www.wattspub.co.uk
or e-mail: bookshop@enterprise.net for details.

To order please quote title, author and ISBN
and your full name and address.
Cheques and postal orders should be made payable to 'Bookpost plc.'
Postage and packing is FREE within the UK
(overseas customers should add £1.00 per book).

Prices and availability are subject to change.